Mallory Goes GReen!

To schools and classrooms around the
country that are going green.
Every little bit makes a big difference.
Keep up the good work!
—L. B. F.

For my Aunt Charlene, who started me on
the path to being green.
—J. K.

MALLORY GOES GREEN!

by Laurie Friedman

illustrations by Jennifer Kalis

MINNEAPOLIS

CONTENTS

A WORD FROM MALLORY

My name is Mallory McDonald, like the restaurant but no relation, age almost 10, and I just switched my lifelong favorite color from purple to green.

If you're wondering why, I'll tell you. I switched from purple to green because I'm going green!

That's right! I, Mallory McDonald, am jumping on the eco-bandwagon.

And I'm not the only one who's doing it. People everywhere are doing things to make our planet a cleaner place to live.

It's called *going green*, and now Fern Falls Elementary is doing it too. Last week at an assembly, our principal, Mrs. Finney, announced that our school is officially *going green*. She said we're all going to take part in a program to improve our community.

Once she said that, everybody I know had something to say about going green.

My teacher, Mr. Knight, said our class is going to be learning a lot about going green. My mom said it might take some time to get used to going green. My best friend, Mary Ann, said going green sounds like a fine idea, but she does NOT think it means I have to switch my favorite color.

I say I can't wait to go green. When my cat, Cheeseburger, was a kitten, I found her and saved her. I loved saving something little, like a cat. But I can't wait to save something big, like a planet.

When it comes to going green, there's only one thing I have to say . . .

Sign me up!

AN ANNOUNCEMENT

"Good morning, class!" Mr. Knight holds the door open as the students of Room 404 walk inside. He waits patiently while everyone puts away coats and gets out pencils and notebooks. When everyone is seated, Mr. Knight smiles.

"Class, I have an announcement," he says.

"Maybe he's getting married," whispers Mary Ann. "And we'll get to be flower girls."

Just thinking about the girls in my class walking down the aisle behind Mr. Knight makes me want to laugh. I press my lips together so I don't. Even though Mr. Knight is in a good mood, I know he won't be for long if I start laughing.

"Class," says Mr. Knight. "Fern Falls Elementary is going green. Mrs. Finney told you a little bit about going green and what it means in the assembly last week. We're going to be discussing it more in class, and I'm going to tell you about an exciting project that everyone at Fern Falls Elementary will be participating in."

I can't wait to get to the exciting project, but I actually do want to learn more about going green. If you ask me, the idea of making our world a cleaner place is a great one.

Mr. Knight writes the words *Going Green* on the blackboard behind him.

"The word *green* has become symbolic for environmental awareness," says Mr. Knight. "When people talk about *going green*, what they mean is that they're looking for ways in their everyday lives to help protect the environment."

I sit back in my chair and listen while Mr. Knight keeps talking.

"Earth has been around for 4.5 billion years," he says.

"That's a lot of years!" April says without raising her hand.

Usually, Mr. Knight gets mad if you don't

raise your hand before you speak. But this time he doesn't.

"That's right, April. Earth has been here a long time, and if we want to keep it around for a long time to come, it's up to us to make it happen. We all have to find ways to save energy, create less pollution, reduce trash, and use less water and electricity. I'd like everyone to take a moment and think of things you can do to live a *greener* lifestyle. Any ideas?"

I think about my own habits. I use water for a lot of things. Brushing my teeth. Taking bubble baths. Washing Cheeseburger. I raise my hand. "I could stop bathing my cat," I say.

I hear lots of *ooohs* and *PUs*. Arielle and Danielle hold their noses like they'd rather waste water than have a stinky cat.

Mr. Knight smiles. "Mallory, I don't think you have to stop bathing your cat entirely, but you could give her shorter baths and perhaps do it less frequently. Nice idea. Any more?"

C-Lo, aka Carlos Lopez, the cute boy who moved this year from Mexico to Fern Falls and who happens to sit in the seat next to me and who also happens to be Mary Ann's boyfriend (but only because she got to him before I did) nods like he likes my idea.

Then he raises his hand. "Maybe we could all take shorter showers and turn the water off while we're brushing our teeth."

Mr. Knight nods like he approves. "Great ideas, Carlos. Anyone else?"

Hands start going up all over the room.

"You can turn out the lights when you leave a room," says Joey.

"You can recycle paper, glass, plastic, and aluminum," says Pamela.

"You can use fluorescent lightbulbs, which save a lot of energy," says Pete.

"You can print things on the backs of pages so you don't waste paper," says Hannah.

Mr. Knight writes the words *Environmental Assignment* on the board. "I would like all of you to make a list of three things you can do at home to make a difference."

I take out a piece of paper and start writing. I personally can't wait to go green.

I plan to stop making so much garbage,
say *no* to bottled water, and turn off the
lights whenever I can.

I sign my name on the top of my paper.
Thinking of three things to do to save the
planet was easy. Come to think of it, I can
think of three things Mom, Dad, and Max
can do too. I start making another list. My
hand is moving almost as fast as my brain.

Mallory McDonald's List of Things
Her Family Can Do to Go Green

Mom- Stop drinking coffee so you don't
waste paper filters or electricity.

Dad-Stop reading the newspaper (save
a tree!) and get the news online.

Max -Stop watching so much TV (especially
the Sports Channel) and save power.

Mr. Knight walks over to my desk and looks down at my list. "Mallory, I'm impressed and happy to see how many ideas you have."

I smile proudly. "I can't wait to go green," I tell Mr. Knight. "And I can't wait for my family to go green with me."

"That's great," says Mr. Knight. "But people usually like to get involved when they're making changes. You might want to talk with your family about things they'd like to do."

Then he looks at the whole class. "Everyone, I'd like you to remember that whatever you put on your list are things I'd like you to stick to and see if you can convince your family to stick to. Remember, change isn't always easy."

Maybe Mr. Knight thinks going green will be hard, but I don't, and I don't see why my family will either. I start imagining the changes that are going to take place at 17 Wish Pond Road, but Mr. Knight interrupts my thoughts.

"OK, everyone, I promised to tell you about an exciting project."

Everyone claps like they can't wait to hear all about it. I know everyone is excited about going green, but for some reason, I'm extra excited about it. I clap so loudly my hands hurt and I let out a whistle.

Mr. Knight starts explaining. "Last week in assembly, Mrs. Finney told you all that Fern Falls Elementary is going green. To kick off our efforts, we're going to have a Green Fair. Each class is going to come up with a project that will help Fern Falls Elementary become more environmentally friendly. All the projects will be presented at the Green Fair."

Mr. Knight pauses. I wish he'd hurry. I can't wait to hear what he has to say.

"Each class will be selecting a representative who will meet with Mrs. Finney and be in charge of coordinating the class project," says Mr. Knight. "I'd like a volunteer. Who would like to be our class representative?"

I would *love* to be!

I raise my hand so high that I feel like my arm might come out of its socket. Just in case Mr. Knight doesn't see my hand, I raise the other one too.

I can see Arielle and Danielle looking at me like I'm a *two-hands-in-the-air* freak, but I don't care. I really want to be our class representative. I pretend I'm at the wish pond on my street. I squeeze my eyes shut and make a wish. *I wish Mr. Knight will pick me.*

I think Mr. Knight can tell how much I want the job, because he does.

"Mallory, the job is yours. You start tomorrow. There's a committee meeting in the morning with Mrs. Finney."

I give Mr. Knight my biggest *thanks-for-picking-me* smile. Then I imagine myself raising my right hand, and I make a pledge:

I, Mallory McDonald, officially pledge to be the best class representative ever.

THE THREE Rs

"No time for breakfast!" I tell Mom. I grab a banana from the bowl on the kitchen table and race out the door. There's no way I'm going to be late for my first-ever committee meeting.

I'm so excited to get started. I have to keep myself from running into the library where the meeting is being held.

"Take your seats please." Mrs. Finney

calls the first meeting of the FFEC, otherwise known as the Fern Falls Environmental Committee, to order.

I look down at my first committee meeting outfit.

Green leggings and T-shirt.

Check.

Notebook made from recycled paper.

Check.

Reusable water bottle.

Check.

If you ask me, I look like the best class representative ever.

I look around the room. It's filled with kids from different classes. I see Katie, a third-grade girl I know, and Nick from second grade. I smile at two first graders.

Winnie is in the back of the room. There's an empty seat next to her. I take it and smile at her, but she doesn't smile back.

Anatomy of a Green Committee Member

organic sun hat

green t-shirt

organic cookies 0% 0

Guide to Recycling

recycled paper notebook

reusable water bottle

green leggings

100% organic cotton socks

"So you're the sixth-grade representative?" I ask her.

"Don't think I'm going to be nice to you just because we're on some stupid committee together." Winnie shakes her head like just the idea of it is stupid. "And what's with that ridiculous outfit?"

I look down at my notebook like I'm ignoring what Winnie said. What's ridiculous is that she thinks this committee is stupid. I'm glad I'm on it, and she should be too.

Sometimes just thinking about Winnie makes me feel like I drank a glass of spoiled milk. I get why Joey and Mary Ann try to be nice to her. She's Joey's sister and Mary Ann's stepsister. They have to live with her. But what I don't get is why my brother, Max, likes spending all of his free time with her.

It's something I'm going to have to figure out later because Mrs. Finney says she's ready to begin. I open my notebook and write my name on the inside cover.

"Good morning, students." Mrs. Finney smiles warmly, like she's glad we're all here.

For a principal, I think she's really nice.

Mrs. Finney picks up a piece of chalk and writes three big Rs on the board. "Last week in assembly, you all heard a little about going green and what it means. You've also discussed it in your classrooms. Today, I want to talk about the three Rs. Does anybody know what they stand for?"

"Really, really, really boring," Winnie whispers under her breath.

Winnie might think the three Rs are really, really, really boring, but I don't. I read about them last night, and I think they're really, really, really important.

I raise my hand before anyone else has a chance to. "Reduce. Reuse. Recycle," I say.

"Very good, Mallory." Mrs. Finney writes *reduce*, *reuse*, and *recycle* on the board. "These three important ideas are what this committee is all about. Reducing the amount of waste we make. Reusing materials. And recycling items that cannot be reused."

Mrs. Finney smiles like she likes the idea behind the three Rs. "Our job as members of this committee is making sure that Fern Falls Elementary finds good ways to *reduce*, *reuse*, and *recycle*. In fact, the three Rs are going to be the theme of our upcoming Green Fair."

Mrs. Finney walks around the room and passes out sheets of paper. I look down at the one she hands me.

FERN FALLS ENVIRONMENTAL COMMITTEE's 3 Rs
REDUCE, REUSE, RECYCLE

Get in the Act by Helping
Your Class **GO GREEN** . . .

Going green protects our future.
Right now in schools and classrooms.
Every little bit counts.
Each thing we do makes a difference.
Now is the time to act!

"Students, going green and finding ways to reduce, reuse, and recycle is something we all must participate in. As members of this committee, it is going to be your job to lead your classrooms in doing this. Today, I want to tell you just how you will be helping."

Everyone starts talking to everyone else. "I can't wait to hear how we will be helping," I say to Winnie. She yawns like the idea of helping is enough to put her to sleep.

Mrs. Finney claps her hands. When the room is quiet, she continues. "Fern Falls Elementary is going to have a Green Fair. Every class will present a project on how they plan to reduce, reuse, or recycle at school. As members of this committee, you will be in charge of leading your class in developing this project. You will be responsible for presenting the project to the other classrooms and the teachers and parents at the Green Fair."

She passes around a schedule and another handout called *50 Ways to Go Green.* "There are many ways your class can get involved. You can use this handout to get started. But I hope you will all work with your classes to come up with ways to reduce, reuse, and recycle."

I read through the handout and then put it into the pocket of my notebook. I can already think of a great way . . . no, scratch that. I can think of a fantastic way my class can get involved. I start scribbling notes.

"Students, I'd like you to take some time and think about going green. You can read about it online or check out books in the library. I'd like you all to prepare a short presentation to give to your classes next week. You should plan to tell them about the three Rs, the Green Fair, and start a discussion about the project your class will do for the fair."

Mrs. Finney looks at her watch. "It's time to go back to your classrooms. Good luck going green. I want to thank each one of you for doing your part in making our school community a more environmentally friendly place."

When Mrs. Finney dismisses us, everyone starts talking at the same time. "I'm so excited about all of this!" I say to Winnie. "I already have a supercool idea for my class project."

Winnie stands up and stretches like she just finished listening to a boring lecture. "I think you need to chill out. No one your age should be so excited about a class project."

I pick up my notebook. I don't care that Winnie thinks I'm too excited about a project. The truth is . . . I am excited about it and I think my class will be too.

The only thing I'm not excited about is that I have to wait until next week to tell them what I have in mind.

THE GREEN POLICE

I, Mallory McDonald, have spent a lot of time lately learning about going green. I have learned that everyone needs to do their part. This weekend, I, Mallory McDonald, am planning to make sure that happens.

When I walk into the kitchen, Mom and Dad and Max are already at the table.

As class representative for the Green Fair, I'm not giving my official presentation to my class until next week, but I can see that my family could use a little lesson on going green too.

I set my notebook down on the kitchen table and tap my spoon on the side of my milk glass.

Everyone looks at me. I clear my throat. "Going green is important," I tell my family. "You all have to do your part."

I look at Mom who is drinking a cup of coffee. "Every time you make coffee, you waste a paper filter and electricity. If you stop drinking coffee, it would be good for the environment."

I start writing on a sheet of paper in my notebook. Then I rip it out. "I'm writing you up for wasting paper and electricity," I say as I hand Mom a ticket.

I see Mom look at Dad like she's not quite sure what to say, but I don't give her a chance to talk. I point to Dad's newspaper. "Every morning you read a

newspaper and throw it away. That's a lot of wasted paper. You could start getting your news online."

I start scribbling and hand Dad a ticket.

Then I look at Max who is sipping his juice box. "Juice boxes are a BIG waste of packaging. And watching the Sports Channel on TV all the time is a big waste of electricity. You should be watching it at the end of the day and get all the scores at once."

I hand Max a ticket.

He wads it up into a ball and tosses it in the direction of the trash can. "I like this kind of juice, and I like watching the Sports Channel. Anyway, who made you the Green Police?" Max looks at Mom and Dad like he could use their help.

Mom clears her throat. "Mallory, I'm really proud of all your efforts to get everyone to go green. But I think we're going to need to spend some time as a family discussing ways that we all want to help out."

I shake my head. "But that's just the thing. We don't have time. We have to save the world before it's too late."

I look at my watch. "I know you'd all love to keep talking about his, but I have to go next door to return the sweater I borrowed from Mary Ann. I promised I'd bring it back this morning so she can wear it today."

"If you want to move next door, I'll help you pack," says Max.

I ignore Max, grab my notebook and Cheeseburger, and walk next door to the Winstons' house.

When I ring the bell, Grandpa Winston answers the door. "Hello, Mallory," he says with a big smile. "I'm glad to see you."

"I'm glad to see you too," I say to Grandpa Winston. Then I point to the porch light. "But I'm not glad to see that your light is still on in the middle of the morning." I take out my notebook and start writing. "I don't want to do this, but

I'm afraid I have to give you a ticket for wasting electricity."

Grandpa Winston looks down at the piece of paper I give him. He seems a little surprised. "I'll be sure and turn the light off," he says softly.

"Good work," I tell him as I step inside.

"Mallory!" Colleen says my name like she's happy to see me. "I'll get Mary Ann. I know she was waiting for you to bring her sweater back."

I hand the sweater to Colleen. I don't know why Mary Ann needs it. "Colleen," I say before she has a chance to go get Mary Ann. "It's really hot in here. You are using more heat than you need." I start scribbling in my notebook. "I'm sorry, but I'm going to have to give you a ticket for wasting electricity."

Colleen, who is always talkative, is quiet.

She looks down at the ticket in her hand. "I'll get Mary Ann," she says.

"Mallory!" Mary Ann and Joey come to the door together. "We were watching TV in the family room. Want to watch with us?"

"I'd love to watch TV," I tell my friends. "But there's something I need to do first."

My friends look like they can't imagine what I'd rather do than watch TV with them.

I start writing in my notebook. "Whenever you leave a room, you should turn off the lights, any appliances, and especially the TV." I hand them each a ticket for being wasteful.

Mary Ann frowns at her ticket.

"What's with the tickets?" asks Joey. "Why do we have to turn off the TV? We're going right back to watch it."

I ignore Joey's questions and turn my head to the side. "Is that water I hear?"

Mary Ann nods. "Winnie is taking a shower."

I think for a second. I heard that same noise when I came in.

I start writing. "You can give this to Winnie," I say as I hand a ticket to Joey. "Please tell her that long showers waste water."

Mary Ann goes into the family room and turns off the TV. "Maybe we'll watch TV another time," she says.

I shake my head like what I'm about to say might be hard for them to understand. "I know it's not easy. But we all have to do our part to save the world's resources."

Mary Ann shrugs. "Some things are definitely not easy," she says. She goes back into the family room, and Joey follows her.

I scoop up Cheeseburger and start walking home.

Even though my family and friends didn't seem to like getting tickets, I know they're happy they learned what they can do to save our planet.

"Next time I see a police officer, I'm going to thank him," I tell my cat.

I had no idea how hard it is to get people to do the right thing.

MALLORY TAKES CHARGE

I'm never the first one in the kitchen. It's usually Mom. But when she walks in this morning, I look up at the clock. I've already been here for an hour.

Mom looks surprised to see me. She looks even more surprised when she sees the mess on the kitchen table. It's covered with pens, note cards, and papers.

"Mallory, what's going on?" she asks.

"Today is the day I'm giving my presentation to my class about the Green Fair."

Mom knows how much preparation I've been doing. "I want this presentation to be really good," I tell her. "I'm trying to be the best class representative ever."

Mom hugs me. "I'm sure you'll be great."

Max walks into the kitchen and looks at the table. "Here's some advice if you want to be great. Keep it short. No one wants to listen to you."

"Max!" Mom says his name like she doesn't like what he just said.

He ignores her and pushes a pile of papers toward me. "Can you at least move some of this stuff so we can put something on the table that we can eat?"

There are only three things my brother thinks about: what he puts in his stomach, baseball, and Winnie.

I hold my hands up and wiggle my fingers in front of Max. "How do you expect me to move all this stuff when my nails are still wet?" I look down at my bright green fingertips. "Like the color?"

I ask Mom. "It matches my presentation."

Mom smiles at me. "The color is perfect."

Max grabs a juice box out of the refrigerator.

I give the juice box in Max's hand an *I-don't-approve* look. "I thought you were going to stop using individual packaging, which is very wasteful."

Max rolls his eyes. "You shouldn't be telling me what to do. You look like our front yard."

I look at my reflection in the oven door. Even though I'm dressed head to toe and down to my fingertips in green, I don't look like a yard. I look like someone who is seriously into going green. "Going green is important," I tell Max. "Everyone needs to do their part."

Max looks down at the table.

"Including you. I see a lot of wasted paper there."

I can't believe my brother is picking the day I'm giving an important presentation to give me a hard time. I pick up a piece of paper off the table. "I didn't waste anything. These papers are part of a VIP, which in case you don't know, is short for a Very Important Presentation."

I wave a sheet of paper in front of my brother's face. "And if you'd take the time to look, you would see that I wrote on the fronts *and* the backs."

Mom takes waffles out of the freezer and pops some into the toaster. "Max, it would be nice if you would help Mallory gather her things while she's waiting for her nails to dry."

Max starts stuffing papers into my backpack.

I hold up my hand to get him to stop and point to Dad's briefcase. "The presentation materials go in the briefcase. Dad said I could borrow it."

Max shakes his head like the idea of me using a briefcase is the craziest thing he's ever heard.

But I don't care. If I'm going to be in charge of my class project, I want to look like I'm in charge.

When the table is paper-free, Mom puts waffles, syrup, and milk on it. Dad walks into the kitchen with the newspaper.

Dad looks at his watch. "Why don't you tell us a little bit about your presentation before you and Max leave for school."

I look at the clock, and then I take a big sip of milk and put my glass down. "Sorry Dad, but it's a big secret. My class is going to be the first to find out what we're doing for the Green Fair. The only thing I can tell you is I have a great idea and my class is going to LOVE it."

I stand up and grab the empty milk carton. "Mr. Knight wants us to bring these into school. He says he's not sure what we will use them for but that they should be good for something." I sling my backpack over my shoulder.

Dad puts his hand on my arm as I start to leave. He gives me a father-knows-best look. "Mallory, I'm sure your idea is a good one, but just make sure you listen to everyone else's ideas as well."

I kiss Dad good-bye and race out the door. What I'm sure of is that my idea isn't just a good one . . . it's a great one! And when my class hears it, they're not even going to want to think about any other ideas.

PRESENTATION TIME

I look at my watch for what must be the three millionth time. This has officially been the longest day in the history of Fern Falls Elementary. In my opinion, Mr. Knight did not make a good choice when he decided I would make my presentation at the *end* of the day.

I don't know how I made it through math and spelling and social studies.

"So are you going to tell us what your project idea is?" Pamela asks me at lunch.

"Puh-leeeze!" says Mary Ann. "We really want to know."

I press my thumb and forefinger together and draw a line with them in front of my mouth like my lips are zipped. I'm

not giving away anything. Not to Pamela.
Not even to Mary Ann.

During science, Mr. Knight asks us to
open our books. I look at my watch. I think
that makes three million and one times.
I cross my toes that it will be my turn
when he gets through talking about rock
formations.

Finally, the time arrives. "Class, we're
going to end our day with something
special. As you all know, Mallory is our
class representative on the environmental
committee, and today, she has prepared a
special presentation."

Mr. Knight nods at me like the floor is
mine.

I pick up my briefcase and walk to the
center of the room to talk to my class. I
open my briefcase and take out my note
cards. I begin with note card #1.

"Fern Falls Elementary is going green."

On to note card #2. "It is exciting that we are, because it is very important to help clean up our world and our school and make it a healthier place for everyone."

I look down at note cards 3, 4, and 5. I have a lot more prepared to say about the environment. But I think about Max's advice about keeping it short. Plus, my class has already heard from Mr. Knight and Mrs. Finney how important it is for us all to go green.

I decide to skip those cards and go straight to what I really came to say.

"As you all know, Fern Falls Elementary is having a Green Fair. The theme of the fair is the three Rs: *Reduce, Reuse,* and *Recycle.* Every class has to come up with a project that they are going to do at school that either reduces, reuses, or recycles the trash that we make at Fern Falls Elementary. The projects will be presented the night of the fair."

Everyone starts talking at once like they have ideas about the project our class is going to do. A few kids raise their hands.

"You can put your hands down," I say. "I will probably answer your questions, and if you still have some when I'm done, then you can ask them."

Danielle rolls her eyes. "You're not the teacher," she mumbles.

I ignore her because it's kind of like I am the teacher. I'm the class representative, so I'm the one in charge. "I know you're all excited about our project for the fair, and I am too. In fact, I'm very, very, very excited because I have a great idea for our class project."

If I had a drum, now would be a good time to roll it. I take a deep breath before I tell the class my idea. "For the Green Fair, we're going to . . ."

"Don't we all get to decide what we're going to do?" Arielle asks without raising her hand.

I ignore Arielle's question since I already said no questions. "For the Green Fair, our class is going to design and sell *Going Green* T-shirts. They will be so cute. We can take orders, and everyone can buy them. Then we can donate the money we make to an organization that is committed to improving the environment."

I don't even wait for everyone to clap. Instead, I keep talking. "There are lots of organizations we can choose from. I've already done some research on the Internet. I know you are all just as excited about this as I am. We should get started immediately."

I smile at my class. I feel warm and glowing on the inside. I nod at everyone so they know that it's their turn to clap or whistle or do whatever they want to do to show me how much they like my idea.

But there's no clapping or whistling or anything else.

"I don't like that idea," says Pete without raising his hand.

"Neither do we," say Arielle and Danielle like they're one person and not two.

"Designing T-shirts doesn't have anything to do with the three Rs," says Zoe.

"You're totally missing the point of the project," says Danielle.

Pamela shakes her head like she doesn't want to say what she's about to say. "Mallory, making T-shirts doesn't reduce, reuse, or recycle anything. That's what this project is supposed to be about."

"We could plant a garden," says Grace.

"Or collect and recycle bottles and cans," says Zack.

Kids start talking all around the room.

This was not at all the reaction I expected.

I give Mary Ann a *you're-my-best-friend-so-please-tell-everyone-how-much-you-love-love-love-my-T-shirt idea* look. But she just shrugs her shoulders and twirls her hair around her finger. I look at Joey to see if he will help me, but he's doodling something on his notebook.

I'm not sure why they picked now to twirl and doodle. I just need to explain my idea a little more, and everyone will love it.

But before I have a chance to explain, the bell rings.

"Class, we will continue this discussion on Monday," says Mr. Knight. "Everyone will have a chance to share their ideas, and then we will vote on the project."

When Mr. Knight finishes talking, everyone starts grabbing books and backpacks and heading out the door. I pick up my things to leave, but Mr. Knight stops me. "Mallory, I appreciate the work and thought you put into your presentation. I know you are very excited about being on this committee. Not only do I want you to think about your idea for the project and if it focuses on reducing, reusing, and recycling, but as class representative, I also want you to think about the importance of being open to other people's ideas. Do you understand what I mean?"

I nod my head like I get it.

He smiles. "Good, then we'll discuss the project more on Monday."

I put my backpack on my back and pick up my briefcase. I understand what Mr. Knight means about how important it is to be open to other people's ideas, but I think what he doesn't understand is that what my class needs to do is be open to my idea because it's a really good one.

And on Monday, I'm going to show them just how good it is.

ON THE BALL

I turn off the faucet in the bathroom sink while Max brushes his teeth.

"Hey! What are you doing?" He tries to turn the water back on, but I turn off the faucet. Then I start writing. "I'm giving you a ticket for wasting water."

Max rips up his ticket and dumps it in the trash. "This Green Police business is getting old. I'm going next door."

I don't even have time to say, "*Have fun*" or "Did you waste all that water just so your breath would be fresh for Winnie?" before Max is already down the hall and out the door.

I walk into the kitchen. Usually Mary Ann and Joey come over on Saturday nights. They know the pizza is here, but there are no signs of them anywhere.

My babysitter Crystal walks into the kitchen with the extra-large pizza box that was just delivered. Then she opens up a package of paper plates.

I start writing. "Sorry." I give my babysitter a ticket. "Paper plates are a waste."

Crystal reads the ticket, and then she laughs. "Mallory, you can't give tickets to people." She folds up the ticket and sticks it into her pocket. Then she turns her attention to the pizza box. "Where is everybody? We're definitely going to need help eating this."

"Max is next door with Winnie," I mumble.

Crystal peers into her crystal ball that she always brings with her and laughs. "I should have seen that one. But what I can't see is where Mary Ann and Joey are. They're always here on Saturday night."

My friends having FUN without me

She rubs her ball. "I don't see any sign of them."

That makes two of us. And it's been like that ever since I started to go green. "I guess they're busy tonight," I tell Crystal.

She doesn't look convinced. "Is everything OK? The three of you are usually inseparable." Crystal takes a slice of pizza out of the box and puts it on a paper plate. She slides it toward me. "Is there anything you'd like to talk about?"

I stuff my mouth with pizza. Someone should give Crystal a T-shirt that says *I switched my job from babysitter to therapist.* "Thanks, but I don't feel like talking."

Crystal looks concerned. "Mallory, if you don't tell me, I'm going to look into my ball and find out." She smiles at me like she really wants to know.

I push my pizza away. I don't feel like eating, and I don't feel like talking either.

Crystal puts her arm around me and steers me to the couch.

She pats it like she's giving me an invitation to sit down. Then she props her crystal ball up on the coffee table and gives it another rub. "Mallory McDonald, let's see if we can figure out what's going on with you."

Sometimes Crystal and her fortune-telling are kind of annoying, but tonight, I could use some help. Things really haven't been so great lately. Ever since I was picked to be class representative, I'd say they've been downright crummy.

Crystal props a pillow behind my back and tells me to breathe deep and relax. "Do you feel better?" she asks.

"Not really," I tell her.

Crystal takes a little bell out of her purse and rings it lightly. "This is supposed to be soothing," she says after a few minutes. "Now do you feel better?"

I shake my head. I still don't.

"We better go with a more traditional approach," says Crystal. "Why don't you tell me what's bothering you."

"I'm not even sure where to start," I say.

Crystal rubs the sides of her head, and then she pulls the crystal ball into her lap and turns it from side to side. She's quiet for a long time while she turns her ball.

"Do you see something?" I ask her.

"Hmmm, it's strange," she says. "All I can see is green. Everything inside my ball is green." She looks at me. "Mallory, are you thinking about dying your hair green?"

I definitely don't have any plans for green hair, but I think I know why everything in Crystal's ball is green. I think back to the day that Mr. Knight picked me to be our class representative for the Green Fair. That's when all my troubles started.

"Now I see Fern Falls Elementary . . . and your house," says Crystal. "Is there something going on at school and home that I should know about?"

I take a deep breath. Then I tell Crystal about going green and the assignment Mr. Knight gave us to try to live a greener lifestyle. "I've tried to get Mom and Dad and Max and all my friends to make some changes, but every time I try to tell them what to do, it's like they don't want to listen to me. I don't think they care about going green."

Crystal is quiet for a minute like she's

thinking. She pulls a piece of paper from her back pocket and unfolds it. "Mallory, am I the first person to get one of these?"

I shake my head *no*.

"That's what I thought," says Crystal. She frowns. "Mallory, you can't tell people what to do. Just because they don't want to give up things they love or do something in a way that might not be convenient or comfortable for them, it doesn't mean they think going green is unimportant. Maybe there are other things they will do."

"But I'm having problems at school too."

I tell Crystal about my idea for the Green Fair and how no one in my class wants to do it. "It's a great project. I've done tons of work on it. I'm supposed to be the one in charge, and I feel like no one will even listen to me. Even Mary Ann and Joey seem like they don't like my idea."

I pet Cheeseburger who is curled up next to me. "Monday at school, my class is going to vote on what project we're going to do at the fair. I really want them to vote for my project."

Crystal is quiet.

"Do you think no one will vote for my project because they're upset that they didn't think of the idea?" I ask.

Crystal doesn't answer right away.

"Maybe you need to look into your crystal ball, and once you see how cute everyone at Fern Falls Elementary looks wearing the T-shirts, you will understand what a great idea it is," I say.

Crystal takes a deep breath and puts her crystal ball back on the table. "Mallory, it sounds to me like you're *telling* people how to go green without *asking* for their input. If you want people to support your ideas, you need to make them part of the process." She looks at me like she's old and wise and I'm young and stupid. "Do you understand what I'm saying?"

I ignore Crystal's question. "Can you please look into your crystal ball and tell me what I need to do to get people to vote for my idea on Monday?" I ask.

Crystal puts her hands on my shoulders. "Mal, I don't need to look into the ball to know what you should do. You need to work with other people to make this project happen."

Crystal pats me on the head like I'm a puppy. "Why don't you talk to your friends next door? I'm sure if you ask them nicely, they will be happy to work with you."

I take a deep breath. Maybe Crystal is right.

Maybe if I ask them nicely, they will vote for me and get other people to vote for me, and before long, everyone at Fern Falls Elementary will be wearing my T-shirts.

I don't know why I didn't think of it myself. That's exactly what I need to do.

I reach across the couch and hug Crystal. After I'm done making T-shirts for my school, I'm going to make one for Crystal that says *World's Smartest Babysitter.*

OPERATION
ASK NICELY

I sit down at the desk in the kitchen and click on the computer. It's time to put Operation *Ask Nicely* into action. I've been thinking about how to do it ever since Crystal and I had our talk last night, and I think I've come up with the perfect plan.

I cross my toes and start typing. I sure hope this works.

Subject: Class Project
From: malgal
To: chatterbox

Dear Mary Ann,

I don't think I told you last week that I thought your outfit on Monday was REALLY cute. I also LOVED what you wore on Tuesday, Wednesday, and Thursday. Your hair looked GREAT on Friday. Actually, it looked great, great, great. But you ALWAYS look great. By the way (in case you forgot), tomorrow in class we are going to vote for the Green Fair project. Will you please tell everyone what a great project making T-shirts is? Remember this: You love T-shirts. You are ALWAYS welcome to borrow any of mine. Plus, you are my BEST friend, and if you want to borrow pants or shoes or anything else, you can borrow those too. So, if anyone asks, just say: VOTE FOR MALLORY!

Thanks so much! I knew I could count on you.

Big, huge hugs and kisses,
Mallory

When I'm done writing to Mary Ann, I start on an email to Joey.

Subject: Class Project
From: malgal
To: boardboy

Dear Joey,

I saw you skateboarding this weekend. You looked F-A-N-T-A-S-T-I-C! Wow! You have gotten really good. You will probably be on a skateboarding team someday. You will definitely be the best one on the team. How cool is that? I mean it. You are soooooo good. Also, tomorrow, do you think you could tell everyone at school to vote for making T-shirts for the Green Fair? If you're not sure what to say, just say this: "Everyone, Mallory's idea of making T-shirts for the Green Fair is a great idea. What are we waiting for? Vote for Mallory!"

Thanks so much,
Mallory

P.S. I will be happy to make T-shirts for your skateboarding team (which you will definitely be on because you are so F-A-N-T-A-S-T-I-C!!!).

I push the *send* button. I hope I hear back from them soon. Tomorrow at school, I just want everyone to vote for my idea. And with Mary Ann's and Joey's help, I think they will. I wonder how long it will take to hear from them. I stand up, stretch, and eat some crackers.

I check the computer. There's no *You've Got Mail* sign.

I drink a glass of milk and feed Cheeseburger.

Still no mail.

I take a shower, wash my hair, condition my hair, put on my purple-striped pj's, and

paint my nails. When I come back into the kitchen, I check the computer. Still no mail.

Mom walks into the kitchen. "It's bedtime," she says. She starts to click the computer off, but I stop her.

"I'm expecting some important mail," I say.

Max rolls his eyes like nothing I get is important, but I ignore him. "Please Mom, just a few more minutes."

Mom looks at the clock. "Five minutes, then it's bedtime."

I hug Mom. Then I tap my foot. *Write me. Write me. Write me.* Whenever you're waiting for something it seems like it takes forever.

Finally, the three words I've been waiting for arrive. *You've Got Mail.* I click on my inbox.

Subject: Class Project

From: chatterbox and boardboy

To: malgal

Mallory,

Why are you so hung up on T-shirts? There are lots of good ways to save the planet. Remember the three Rs? We don't think making T-shirts has anything to do with the Rs.

Think Rs!

Mary Ann and Joey

P.S. Can I borrow your yellow rainbow T-shirt? Thanks! I know you will think it is a good idea to reuse your T-shirt. Get it? Reuse! (In case you weren't sure, that was from Mary Ann.)

When I'm done reading, I rub my eyes.
I can't believe what I just read. I read it
again. I can't believe my best friends don't
see what a good idea making T-shirts is.
And I can't believe they won't help me,
especially after I asked so nicely.

"Bedtime," says Mom. She clicks off the
computer.

I scoop up Cheeseburger and head to my
room. I put the two of us in bed and turn
out the light. I don't even wait for Mom
and Dad to come tuck me in.

Operation *Ask Nicely*
did not go as planned.

Tomorrow, I'm
going to have to put
Operation *Vote for
Mallory* into place.

ELECTION DAY

Now I know how people who are running
for president must feel. The minute I wake
up, the only thing I can think about is *Vote
for Mallory!*

Today is the day my class decides what
project we're going to do for the Green
Fair, and I'm going to do everything I can
to get them to vote for mine.

I close my eyes and pretend I'm at the

wish pond. I make a wish. *I wish today will be a great day and my class will decide that making T-shirts for the Green Fair is an idea worth voting for.*

I know that's actually two wishes, but it's really just one. Today will be a great day if my class goes along with my idea.

I put Operation *Vote for Mallory* into place as soon as I leave my house.

"Since everyone was having trouble understanding my ideas for the Green Fair, I brought some things to make it easier for everyone to see what a great project making T-shirts will be," I say to Joey and Mary Ann as we walk toward school.

My friends look at each other like they're thinking one thing and I'm thinking another.

"I have designs, committee lists, and ideas for charities."

I reach my arm across my body and pat my backpack. "It's all in the bag. I did everything. Now, the only thing left for everyone else to do is vote for my idea."

"Maybe we should collect and recycle used batteries instead," says Joey.

"Or we could put up signs that say *Don't Wear Fur!*" says Mary Ann.

I shake my head. I don't know why my friends are thinking about batteries or fur when they should be talking about T-shirts. I take a deep breath. Then I tell them something that I know will make them want to vote for my project and get other people to vote for it too. "Since you're my best friends, if the class votes to make T-shirts, you get to be my assistants."

I smile at Mary Ann and Joey and wait for them to smile back and say what a cool project this is and how much they love the idea of being my assistants and that they are going to do everything they can to get everybody to vote for me.

But they don't smile or say anything like that. Mary Ann looks at Joey.

"Mallory, we need to talk to you," says Joey.

I glance at my watch. "We can talk later. The bell is going to ring any minute, and I don't want to be late on Election Day. C'mon!" I say as I run ahead of them.

When I get to my classroom, Mr. Knight is already waiting for everyone to sit down.

"Class, as you all know, this Friday night is the Green Fair. We started a discussion about it last week, and we need to finish it this morning. I know some of you had different ideas on what you think our class project should be. This morning, I'd like to reopen the discussion, and then we will vote to decide what we're going to do."

Just hearing Mr. Knight say the word *vote* makes me excited and nervous at the same time. I know a lot of people in my class, including my best friends, don't like my idea. But I think they will once they hear what I have to say. I raise my hand.

Mr. Knight calls on me.

I take everything I need out of my backpack and walk to the center of the class. I smile at everyone. "I know some of you didn't understand my idea for the Green Fair when I explained it last week."

Arielle and Danielle roll their eyes at each other like they're not the ones who don't get it.

I ignore them and continue. "I brought some things today that will help you understand what I'm talking about."

I show T-shirt designs.

I read committee lists.

I pass around information about different charities.

"It's going to be so much fun to sell T-shirts at school. We can even make

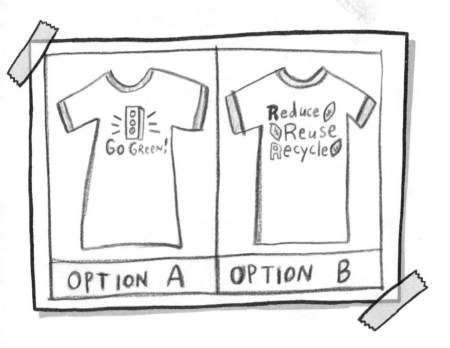

posters and have a *wear-your-green-T-shirts-to-school* day."

I smile again at my class when I'm done explaining. "Now I'm sure you all get what a great project this is." I sit down at my desk and wait for them to clap and cheer. I hope Mr. Knight won't be upset if our classroom is as loud as a rock concert.

But our classroom doesn't sound anything like a rock concert. In fact, the only noise in our classroom is the sound of people raising their hands.

Mr. Knight calls on Arielle.

"Danielle and I think our class project should be decorating recycling bins and putting them in the cafeteria so everyone can recycle their trash at lunch instead of throwing it away."

"I like that idea," says April.

"Me too," says Hannah.

"I think recycling bins in the cafeteria is a perfect idea," says Dawn.

"They'll look really cute," says Zoe.

I raise my hand. I want to say that if they think recycling bins will look cute, I can't wait for them to see my T-shirts. But Mr. Knight doesn't call on me.

He points to Emma.

"I like the idea of making recycling bins too. I think that will be a great thing to have at Fern Falls Elementary," she says.

A lot of people start nodding their heads like they like the idea.

I look at Mary Ann and Joey like I could really use some best friend help. It would be great if one of them would say: *"Hey everyone, recycling bins are nice. But T-shirts are even nicer. Vote for T-shirts. Yeah!"*

But neither one of them says that.

"Class, it's time to vote on our project," says Mr. Knight. He writes the words *recycling bins* and *T-shirts* on the board. "Does anyone have any other ideas that they would like to propose?"

No one does so Mr. Knight calls for a vote. "All in favor of T-shirts, raise your hands."

I cross my toes. "Vote for T-shirts," I mouth across the room to Pamela.

But Pamela doesn't look at me like she's planning to vote for T-shirts. I look at her hand and pretend like I'm at the wish pond. I wish Pamela's hand will go up in the air.

But it doesn't. In fact, the only hand in my classroom that is up in the air is my own. I close my eyes and make another wish. *I wish any hand in this room will go up in the air.* But none do.

"All in favor of recycling bins, please raise your hands," says Mr. Knight.

I watch as hands start popping up all over the room. They go up so fast, I don't

have time to pretend like I'm at the wish pond and wish they didn't. Every hand in the classroom is up.

I feel like I'm surrounded by a sea of raised hands.

Mr. Knight looks at me like he's sorry for what he's about to say. "Class, it looks like our project for the Green Fair is going to be recycling bins."

Even though Mr. Knight didn't come right out and say it, he could have said, "*Mallory, your idea stinks. No one wants any part of it. As far as class representatives go, consider yourself fired.*"

I try to smile like I'm OK with doing recycling bins. But I can't think about recycling bins. All I can think about is how much I wanted to make T-shirts.

I remember how excited I was when Mr. Knight picked me to be on the Fern Falls

Environmental Committee. I couldn't wait to lead my class in their efforts to go green.

I pictured myself working with my classmates on the project that I designed. I pictured myself standing on the stage at the Green Fair telling parents and students and teachers about our great project. I pictured myself saving the planet and making our school a cleaner place.

But I never pictured everyone in my class working on a project that I had nothing to do with.

All of a sudden, my classroom feels hot and too small.

Even though the day just started, I wish it was already over. It's too bad there aren't recycling bins in the cafeteria yet. If there were, I'd get in one.

I would like to be recycled as a girl who has ideas that people actually like.

MALLORY ALONE

Once upon a time there was a beautiful, darling, sweet, smart, perfect, adorable, caring girl. All she wanted to do was help save the planet. So she volunteered to be her class representative for the Green Fair.

It was a truly selfless thing to do. Though saving the planet sounded like a big, difficult thing to some people, it didn't to her. To the contrary, she thought that saving the planet would be as simple as making a few T-shirts. She even came up with some great designs for the shirts.

In her head, she pictured everyone at her school walking around wearing the T-shirts and spreading the word about saving the earth.

But unfortunately, her classmates didn't see things the way she did. They didn't get the whole T-shirt thing. In fact, not only did they NOT want any part of the beautiful, darling, sweet, smart, perfect, adorable, caring girl's ideas, but even worse, they voted against her. Even when the girl tried to explain to them why her ideas were so good, they just said, "Let's do something else."

It was like they all ganged up against her for no reason whatsoever.

Here's the worst part of the story. (Actually there are four worst parts so keep reading.)

Worst part #1: All week long at school, especially every day during lunch and at recess and between subjects and on the way to art and P.E., the only thing anybody was talking about was the class project, and the place they seemed to be talking about it the most was right in front of the poor girl. Everywhere she went, the only words she heard were "recycling bins."

Worst part #2: The awful, mean, cruel, ugly, not clever, boring, mean (I know I used that word already, but it's the right word, so

Happy girls

I'm using it again) girls who thought of the recycling bin idea kept saying to the beautiful, darling, sweet, smart, perfect, adorable caring girl things like, "Ha! Ha! The class liked our idea and not yours." (They didn't say it just like that, but the girl knew they were thinking it.)

Worst part #3: Just because the girl was acting a little sulky (which is totally understandable given the circumstances) at school, her teacher had a talk with her about the importance of learning to work with other people. It was unfair

SAD GIRL

that he talked to her and not the rest of the class when they were the ones that didn't even try to work with her.

Worst part #4: The girl's two best friends whose names start with an M and J (but on top of being beautiful, darling, sweet, smart, perfect, adorable, and caring, the little girl is too polite to

name names)
not only didn't
get everyone
to vote for her
idea, but they
also never
even said to
her that they

Friends who don't care

were sorry they voted for someone else's
idea. Then all week long, they acted like
it was totally no big deal, which made
the girl feel like they had completely
forgotten that they were supposed to be
her best friends.

So, as you can imagine, this little girl
felt rotten and alone the week of the
Green Fair when she should have been
feeling fantastic.

Poor, lonely girl.

THE L WORD

I put Cheeseburger down on the bench beside me and throw a stone into the wish pond. I watch it bounce along the surface and then sink into the water.

The sun is starting to set and I'm glad. This week was the worst week ever. The Green Fair is tomorrow night, and I, Mallory McDonald, officially can't wait for it to be over.

I think about everything that happened this week.

No one in my class voted for my idea. Not even my best friends. Everyone kept talking about the recycling bins right in front of me. And my teacher had his *Mallory-you-really-need-to-learn-how-to-work-with-others* talk with me.

I can feel the tears that I've been holding back all week starting to trickle down my face. I wipe my cheek and try not to think about it.

But it doesn't work. The more I try not to think about things, the more I do. I wanted to be a great class representative and help lead my class in going green, but I feel like there was nothing great about anything I did.

I rub the fur behind Cheeseburger's ears. "You're probably the only one who doesn't think I'm a failure," I say to my cat.

"You can add my name to that list," a voice says from behind me.

I don't have to turn around to know that it's Dad.

He sits down beside me.

"Feel like a doughnut?" Dad places a box of chocolate-covered sprinkle doughnuts beside me. "I won't tell Mom I gave them to you before dinner if you won't tell."

I know Dad is trying to make me smile, but I don't.

He tries again. "I promise to recycle the box when we're done." Dad holds up two fingers scout's honor-style.

It's hard not to smile at the idea of Dad dressed as a Boy Scout. I take a doughnut and eat a tiny bite.

Dad puts his arm around me. "A little birdie told me you were out and that you haven't been yourself lately. I wanted to check on you."

I scratch my head. "Does the little birdie have a name?"

"Actually the little birdie has several names. Joey and Mary Ann told Colleen that you seem a little down. Colleen told Mom and Mom told me."

I look down at my feet. "Good news travels fast around here."

"A lot of people care about you, and that's why I'm here," says Dad.

I shake my head. "Maybe you care about me," I tell Dad. "But no one else does."

Dad looks down at me and shakes his head like I couldn't be more wrong.

Sometimes parents think they know things just because they're parents. But this time, Dad is wrong. He doesn't know what he's talking about.

"Dad, no one in my class liked my idea for the Green Fair. My teacher thinks I didn't do a good job working with others. My best friends are acting like they've forgotten about me. And even though you say you care about me, lately, it seems like you and Mom and Max are sick of me and all my green ideas too." I pull my cat into my lap. "I think Cheeseburger is the only one who's glad I even exist."

Dad pulls me close to him. "Mallory, people might not like some of the things you did or some of your ideas, but it doesn't mean they don't like you."

"But that's the thing," I tell Dad. "I was trying to do the right thing at home and at school. I'm trying to make our planet a cleaner place, and no one wants to help me. I feel like I'm the only one in the world who wants to clean things up."

"Mallory, I don't think anyone is objecting to what you tried to do. I think the problem is how you went about doing it."

Portrait of a Lone cleaner

I pick up a stone. I don't say anything because I'm not sure what to say.

Dad keeps talking. "Everyone wants our planet to be a cleaner place, but people want to have some say in how they go about cleaning it up."

I think about what Mr. Knight said. He and Dad sound a lot alike.

Then I think about my T-shirts. I spent a lot of time designing them. "I just think it would have been great for everyone in my class to have *Go Green* T-shirts," I tell Dad.

"Maybe it would have been," says Dad. "But your classmates wanted to be part of making that decision too. And the same thing goes at home. Mom and Max and I all want to have a greener lifestyle. We want to hear your ideas. But believe it or not, we have some of our own ideas and we want you to listen to those as well."

I look down at the doughnut in my hand. I don't feel like eating it.

"Mallory, I know you've been spending a lot of time at school talking about the three Rs. But I think it's time we talk about a word that starts with *L*."

I don't have to think to know what word Dad is talking about. Mr. Knight used it too. "I guess I haven't been a very good listener lately," I say to Dad.

He nods his head like he agrees with me.

I didn't think I had any left, but more tears trickle down my cheeks. "Everything is a mess," I tell Dad. "My teacher thinks I was a big, fat flop as class representative. My best friends are hardly my best friends anymore. No one in my class liked my ideas, and now, it feels like everyone in my class is on one team and I'm on another. And the Green Fair is tomorrow night, and I'm hardly part of it."

Dad wraps his arms around me. Then he lets go of me and wiggles my ears. "I think it's time to show people that you know how to use these," he says. He gets a serious look on his face. "Mallory, you've got two ears, and there's no time like the present to put them to good use."

I blow my nose into one of the napkins from the doughnut box. "Dad, it's too late. How can being a good listener help me now?"

Dad gives me a big hug. "Mallory, you're very resourceful. Perhaps it will take more than listening to others. I know it seems like things are a mess right now, but I'm sure if you put your head to it, you'll come up with a solution that will make you and everyone around you feel better."

He stands up. "Why don't you take some time to think, and come back to the house when you're ready." Dad kisses the top of my head, and then he leaves.

I throw another stone in the wish pond and watch it sink. I can't imagine what I can do to fix everything.

Whoever thinks it's hard to find a solution to pollution has never tried to solve all of my problems.

HEADS
TOGETHER

"Are you going to eat all those doughnuts by yourself?"

I know who that voice belongs to. I turn around to look at Joey, but when I do, I'm surprised at what I see. Mary Ann is with Joey.

They sit down beside me.

I know my friends didn't come here to eat. "I'm surprised you're here," I say softly.

Joey gives Mary Ann a *you-go-first* look.

"We know you're upset," says Mary Ann. "We don't like seeing you like this."

I feel a big lump in my throat, like I forgot to swallow my doughnut. I wish I could go back in time to when Mr. Knight first picked me to be our class representative. Everything was fine before then. Now, everything is NOT fine. I wish I could have done things differently.

I look down at the wish pond. "Everything is a big mess."

Joey looks around the wish pond. Then he laughs. "I don't see any messes."

I know he's trying to be funny. I pick up a rock and throw it into the water. "You know what I mean. I did a terrible job as our class representative. No one thinks I listened to what they wanted to do. Everyone in our class thinks I stink and so does Mr. Knight."

Joey pretends to sniff the air around us. "I don't smell anything bad? Do you?" he asks Mary Ann.

Joey is trying really hard to make me laugh. But I don't. Nothing seems funny right now. I look down at the box in my lap. If it weren't filled with doughnuts, I could fill the whole thing with my tears. I swallow hard. I really don't want to start crying again.

I pick up a rock and throw it in the wish pond. I think about what Dad said about listening to others. I know I didn't listen to my best friends when they tried to talk to me.

"Ever since this whole recycling thing started, I guess I haven't exactly been the easiest person in the world to be friends with."

Mary Ann nods her head like what I'm saying is true. "Mallory, I'd like to give you a ticket for being the hardest person in the world to be friends with," she says.

Joey gives her a *that-might-not-have-been-the-right-thing-to-say* look.

But Mary Ann keeps going. "You didn't listen to anybody's ideas. Not even mine or Joey's. It was like you only wanted to do what you wanted to do and you didn't even care what anybody else wanted. And those tickets . . ."

I stop Mary Ann before she has time to say more. "I'm really sorry I didn't listen to your ideas and that I tried to tell you how to do things," I say softly to my friends.

Mary Ann throws her arm around my shoulder. "As your best friends, we can't stay mad at you. Apology accepted." She looks at Joey like it's his turn to accept my apology too, which he does.

I take a deep breath. "I feel better knowing that you're not mad anymore, but I still feel bad about our class. I want everyone to know I'm sorry that I didn't listen to their ideas."

"Maybe you should tell them," says Joey.

I shake my head. "It's a lot easier telling you. I don't know what I would say."

Joey looks at Mary Ann. "Maybe we can help you think of something. Isn't that what best friends are for? To help you when you really need help?"

Joey and Mary Ann are such good friends. I can't believe I was mad when they didn't tell everyone to like my T-shirt idea. They're here now, and I could really use their help. "So what do you think I should say to everyone?"

Mary Ann twirls a curl around her finger. "That's a tough one," she says. "But I know we can come up with something."

"We can if we put our heads together," says Joey. "You know what they say . . . three heads are better than one."

I smile. "I thought the saying was that two heads are better than one."

Joey laughs. "If two heads are better than one, then think how good three heads are."

I smile at Joey. The idea of a few extra heads, especially when they belong to my best friends, sounds a whole lot better than one. "Thanks," I tell Mary Ann and Joey.

"Don't thank us yet," says Joey. "We still haven't thought of anything."

I nod like I understand that *thank-yous* will come after we think of something.

3-Headed Wonder

Then I take two doughnuts out of the box and hand them each one.

No one can think on an empty stomach.

TEAMMATES

"Don't worry," Joey says as we walk through the gates of Fern Falls Elementary.

Mary Ann presses my thumbs and forefingers together like she's putting me into a yoga pose. "Breathe deep."

I try to take a deep breath. But it doesn't help.

Mary Ann squeezes my shoulders. "Everybody will love it."

I hope Mary Ann is right and everybody likes what I'm planning to say and do. I think back to last night. Joey and Mary Ann and I stayed up so late and worked so hard. I can't believe how much they helped me. They really are the best friends a girl could have.

When I walk into Room 404, Arielle and Danielle are busy gluing rhinestones onto recycling bins. "We have a lot to do before the Green Fair tonight," Arielle says to me.

Arielle and Danielle aren't the only ones with a lot to do.

I put Operation *Fix Things with My Classmates* into place. I walk up to Mr. Knight's desk. Then I explain to him what I want to do. My voice is almost a whisper. I don't want anyone else to hear what I have to say. At least, not yet.

When I'm done explaining, Mr. Knight nods like he approves. Then he clears his throat.

"Class, Mallory has something that she'd like to say to you. I'd like you all to give her your full attention."

I take a small bag out of my backpack and walk to the middle of the classroom. I've been here a lot lately, but this time, it doesn't feel fun or easy to say what I came to say.

Mr. Knight nods like he's ready for me to begin.

Joey gives me a *you'll-be-fine* look. Mary Ann crosses her fingers on both hands like a good luck sign.

I take another deep breath and get started. "I've already made one speech as class representative about what it means to go green, but today, I want to make another one."

I squeeze the edges of the bag I'm
holding. "I thought going green was about
everybody doing their part to make the
world a cleaner place. We do have to do
that. But what we really need to do is work

together to improve our community. As your class representative for the Fern Falls Environmental Committee, it was my job to make sure we all worked together as a class to come up with a project for the Green Fair."

I shift from one foot to the other. That was the easy part of my speech. What I have to say next is a little more difficult.

"I didn't do a very good job at that. I was so sure that making T-shirts was the perfect project for the Green Fair that I didn't listen to anyone else's ideas. I'm really sorry. No. Scratch that. I'm really, really, really sorry. I just want to say that I think decorating recycling bins to put in the cafeteria is a great idea. I know everyone will love it when we present the idea tonight at the Green Fair."

Then I open up the bag I'm holding. "I made green pins for everyone." I walk around the classroom and start handing out the little green ribbons that Mary Ann and Joey helped me tie and glue onto safety pins last night. "I hope you like them. I wanted everyone to have one. We're all members of the same Green Team. We all need to work together."

I watch as all of my classmates start pinning on their ribbons. "We can all wear the ribbons tonight, if you want to."

Mr. Knight nods like he approves of the idea. Then he looks at everyone. "Class, what do you say? Shall we wear our green pins tonight?"

April raises her hand. "I vote that we wear the green pins."

C-Lo raises his hand. "Me too," he says.

"So do I," says Pamela. She pats her green ribbon and raises her hand. In fact, a lot of people are raising their hands. For the second time this week, I feel like I'm surrounded by a sea of raised hands, but this time I like it.

Even though I loved the idea of making the T-shirts, I like the idea of listening to other people and making sure that they feel good too, even better. I wink at Mary

Ann and Joey who are sitting in the back of the room. I never could have done this without their help.

But when I look at them, I see something besides my best friends in the back of the room. I can't believe I didn't think of it before. It's like a fluorescent, energy-saving lightbulb just went off in my brain.

Mary Ann looks at me like she knows I just thought of something, but she can't imagine what it is. I walk to the back of the class and pick up one of the empty milk cartons that everyone brought in. I hold it up and turn it from side to side. "I read something in my recycling book about turning these into bird feeders."

Dawn grabs the milk carton out of my hand. "Mallory, that's a great idea!"

"How do you turn milk cartons into bird feeders?" Hannah asks.

I think about the diagram in my book. "We could cut out the fronts and paint them and fill them with seeds."

"They would be so cute," says Zoe.

Everyone starts walking over to listen while we talk about bird feeders.

Arielle shakes her head. "I thought we decided to do recycling bins."

"Me too," says Danielle.

"Maybe we can do recycling bins *and* bird feeders." I look at my class. "If everyone likes that idea." Then I look at my teacher. "And if Mr. Knight says we have time."

Mr. Knight rubs his forehead. "Does everybody like the idea of making bird feeders?"

"Vote for Mallory," Pamela says out loud.

Lots of kids clap and smile. C-Lo whistles like he loves the idea.

"Now that everyone is working together, I'm sure we can get it done in a timely manner," says Mr. Knight. "But since the fair is tonight, I think we better skip math this morning so we don't have to rush. Does everybody like that idea?"

Everyone claps and cheers.

"Vote for Mr. Knight," says C-Lo.

Everyone laughs, including my teacher. "Then it's settled," says Mr. Knight. "Get busy. We have a lot to do and not much time to do it."

Everyone starts cutting, painting, and gluing.

I start to pick up a pair of scissors.
Then I put them down. I have something
more important to do than making a
bird feeder. I walk over to Mary Ann and
Joey.

"Thanks for helping me. You're the
two best friends a girl could ever have.
Without you, there wouldn't be a Green
Team."

Joey grins. "Glad we could help."

Mary Ann puts one arm around me and the other one around Joey. "I'm glad we have a Green Team, but I'm even more glad we have a best-friend team."

Joey nods like he agrees, and so do I.

"I couldn't imagine better teammates," I tell my friends.

A FAIR TO REMEMBER

"Everyone, please take your seats. It's time to kick off Fern Falls Elementary's efforts to go green at our first ever Green Fair!" says our principal, Mrs. Finney.

There are lots of cheers and claps and whistles from the audience. Someone even yells out, "Go Green!" like they're at a football game and they're rooting for their team.

"Good evening, everyone," says Mrs. Finney once everyone has taken their seats in the auditorium.

"I like her outfit almost as much as I like ours," Mary Ann whispers into my ear from the seat next to me.

Mary Ann and I aren't the only ones wearing head-to-toe green. So are Mrs. Finney and lots of other people too.

I look around. It's Friday night, and every seat in the place is filled with students, teachers, and parents. There are even people standing in the aisles. I see Mom and Dad sitting in the back. "I've never seen this auditorium so crowded," I say to Mary Ann.

"Or so green," she adds.

Mary Ann is right. It looks like we're sitting on a giant field, not in an auditorium.

"It's cool that so many people care about going green," Joey says from the seat on the other side of me.

I nod. I definitely agree with that.

Mrs. Finney taps on the microphone to get everyone's attention. "Today, I want to *plant* the idea of recycling in all of your heads." Then she laughs. "Just a little green humor."

The audience laughs too. Once they're quiet, she continues.

"Fern Falls Elementary is committed to going green. There are many things that schools can do to provide a more environmentally friendly environment. Here at Fern Falls, we are sticking to what I like to refer to as the three Rs." She points to a giant sign on the stage that lists the three Rs. Then she puts her hand up to her ear like she's waiting to hear what they are.

"Reduce! Reuse! Recycle!" All the
students shout together at the same time.

Mrs. Finney smiles. "I'm glad to see
our students know just what I'm talking
about. All of our classes have been working
on projects that incorporate the ideas of
reducing, reusing, or recycling. Tonight,
each classroom is going to be called up to
the stage and they will present their project
to the audience. It will give us all a sense of

the kinds of things we will be doing at our school in our efforts to go green."

The parents clap even though they don't even know what the projects are yet.

Mrs. Finney taps on the microphone again. "Before we hear from our classes, I'd like to recognize some very important volunteers. One student from each of our classes served on the Fern Falls Environmental Committee as liaisons between the committee and their classrooms. It was their responsibility to lead their classes in organizing tonight's projects.

"Without these special and committed students, tonight would not be possible." Mrs. Finney smiles out into the audience like she's trying to find and personally thank each committee member. "I'm going to call off the names of the committee members. When I call out your name, I'd like you to please rise."

As she reads through the list, students start popping up like popcorn kernels exploding out of the popper at the movies. When Mrs. Finney calls out my name, I stand up with the other kids.

"*Yeah, Mallory!*" mouths Mary Ann. She and Joey smile up at me like they're proud.

I smile. Even though I'm not so proud of how I started out as a committee member, I'm happy about the way things ended up, and I can't wait until we present our project . . . or maybe I should say *projects*. I hope Mrs. Finney won't mind that my class did two.

After she has called out the committee members, Mrs. Finney announces that it is time to start hearing about the projects. She calls on Winnie's class first.

The sixth graders go up on the stage, and Winnie walks up to the microphone. "As our class project, one day per week, we are going to take all of the uneaten food from the cafeteria to a homeless shelter."

There is lots of clapping as different kids in Winnie's class explain exactly what they plan to do.

I can tell the audience likes that project. Even Winnie seems excited about it. I hope they like our projects too.

I try to listen patiently while other classes present their ideas.

The first and second graders are working together to plant a garden on the playground and reuse coffee grounds from the teachers' lounge to fertilize the plants.

The third graders are going to put a chart up in the cafeteria and give sticker stars to people who stop using disposable bags and boxes for their lunches and start using lunch boxes and reusable containers.

The fifth graders are going to put paper recycling bins in all the classrooms and have a contest to see which class recycles the most paper.

Even though there are some great ideas, I can't help being excited to present the ideas my class came up with. When Mrs. Finney finally calls on my class, we're the last one to go.

I look around at all of my classmates, and then lead them up to the stage.

Once we are all together, I take the microphone. "Our class couldn't decide on just one project," I tell the audience. "So we made two."

Everyone in the audience is quiet like they can't wait to hear.

I give the microphone to Danielle. While she explains about the new recycling bins in the cafeteria, Arielle and Pete hold one up so everyone can see.

When Danielle is done explaining, she hands the microphone to Pamela who tells everyone about the bird feeders we made from recycled milk cartons. While she talks, Zoe, April, and Zack walk to the front of the stage and hold up samples for everyone to see.

When we're done, the auditorium fills with applause.

"I think it went great," I whisper to Mary Ann as we sit back down.

"No, it didn't," says Mary Ann. I stop smiling when I see that she's not.

"How do you think it went?" I asked.

Mary Ann breaks out into a big smile. "It went great, great, great!"

Now it's my turn to smile again. I'm so happy everything worked out so well.

Mrs. Finney asks for everyone's attention. The kindergartners go up on the stage and sing a special song about the environment.

When they're done, Mrs. Finney thanks everyone for coming. "Drive home safely," she says. "Or better yet, walk and save some gas!"

"The fair was fantastic!" Mom says as we start to walk out of the auditorium. "I thought your class project turned out perfectly," she says.

"That makes two of us!" Mr. Knight is by my side. "Mallory, I know it wasn't easy being a class leader, but I think you learned a lot and did a great job. I'm very proud of you."

I thank Mr. Knight and walk outside with Mary Ann and Joey. "If tonight could get a grade, I'd give it an A+," I tell my friends.

"I'd give it an A+++," says Mary Ann.

I nod like I agree. "Everything turned out great. And thanks again for all your help. I couldn't have done it without you both."

They smile like they're glad they could help.

As I walk back to Mom's van between my two best friends, I slip my arms through both of theirs. If friends could get a grade, I'd give them both an A+++.

A MEAL TO FORGET

"Dinner in ten minutes!" Mom says.

I say ten minutes is ten minutes longer than I want to wait. One thing about school fairs is that they make you very hungry!

I go to my room, pet Cheeseburger, and wash my hands. I can't believe how well the fair turned out. Everyone really loved our class projects. I can't wait to see how the new recycling bins and bird feeders look around Fern Falls Elementary.

I scoop up Cheeseburger from my bed and walk down the hall. "Something smells good," I say as I sit down.

Mom smiles. "Mallory, tonight I made a special dinner in honor of all your efforts to make the Green Fair such a big success."

Now I'm the one who's smiling. "I'm really proud of the way our class projects turned out."

"You should be," says Mom. Then she puts her arm around me. "I know you had your heart set on T-shirts, but Fern Falls Elementary needs recycling bins, and the bird feeders will be a nice addition to our school too. I'm proud of you for going along with what everyone else wanted to do."

Max rolls his eyes. I know he thinks I've been a pain about this whole going green thing, but tonight, I'm so happy that the fair was a success, that nothing Max does can upset me.

"OK," says Mom. "Everyone sit down. Mallory, close your eyes."

I close my eyes, but not my mouth. It's like it has a mind of its own, and it can't stop smiling. Just knowing Mom made a special dinner for me makes me feel good.

"Ta-da! Open your eyes," says Mom.

But when I do, I can feel my smile disappearing.

Mom puts a big platter of broccoli, spinach, peas, and zucchini in front of me. "It's a green meal in honor of all your work to make the Green Fair so successful."

Mom fills my plate with vegetables. Then she gives me a hug. "I know how

important going green is to you. Now you are doing it at school, at home, and even at the dinner table."

I try to smile like I'm really happy about this green meal, but the truth is, there are a lot of things I like to eat, but NONE of them are green.

"Go on," says Dad. "Eat up! Mom made this meal just for you."

I take a tiny bite of broccoli. I try not to make a face. But I want to save trees, not eat them.

"Mallory, you're very quiet," says Dad.

"Here," says Mom. She spoons more peas onto my plate.

Everyone is watching me. I take a bite of zucchini, and then I eat a forkful of peas.

"Try the spinach," says Mom. "It's delicious."

I take a little bite. If whoever made up the expression *too much of a good thing* were at this meal, I think they'd change it to *too much of a green thing*. I push all of the green things around on my plate. I don't know if I can eat one more bite of anything green.

All of a sudden, Mom, Dad, and Max laugh.

"Look!" Max points to my face. "Mallory is going green!"

I run to the bathroom and look in the mirror. I didn't think people could go green, but I do look kind of green.

When I come back into the kitchen, everyone is still laughing. "Is there anything else for dinner . . . that's not green?" I ask.

Mom walks over and puts her arm around me. "Mallory, we're just teasing you. We know how much effort you've put into going green, and we thought this would be funny."

I shake my head like there's nothing funny about a plateful of green vegetables.

"How about some spaghetti and meatballs to go with your vegetables?"

I can feel the green fading from my face. "That sounds great!" I say. I sit back down and eat every bite of my spaghetti. "It's important not to waste food."

And for once, I can tell Max agrees with me because he eats every bite of spaghetti on his plate too.

When we're done with dinner, Mom puts a big fruit salad on the table. I fill my dessert plate with strawberries, pineapple, and blueberries. I pop a blueberry into my mouth. I feel like there's something I need to say to my family, and now seems like the right time to say it.

"I just want to tell you all that I'm really sorry if I've been kind of a pain lately. I just got so excited about going green that I didn't stop to think about how anybody else felt about it." I push my plate of fruit back. "I know I gave ribbons to everybody in my class for going green. I feel like I should give something to you too. As soon as we're done with dinner, I'm going to make green ribbons for all of you."

"How about instead of giving me a ribbon, you can do my chores?" says Max.

Mom and Dad both give Max a *Mallory-is-not-doing-your-chores* look.

"Mallory, that's a nice idea," says Dad. "But you don't need to make ribbons for us. We're proud of all your efforts to go green, and we think you learned a lot through this experience about how to work with others in accomplishing something."

I'm glad Mom and Dad are proud of me, and I'm really glad that 17 Wish Pond Road and Fern Falls Elementary are more environmentally friendly than they used to be.

I stand up and stretch. "I'm going to get ready for bed."

Mom smiles. "It's been a long day, and you must be exhausted."

When Mom and Dad come into my room to tuck me in, I'm already in bed with Cheeseburger.

Dad bends down and kisses my forehead. "Good night, Sweet Potato." He starts to turn off the light, but I stop him.

"I've been doing some thinking," I say to my parents. "And I have a really good idea for another way to go green."

Before Mom or Dad has time to say I've had enough ideas lately, I tell them what's on my mind. "Since going green is my new favorite activity and green is my new favorite color, I think we should paint my room green."

Mom and Dad look at each other.

I keep talking. "I've already thought it through. We can paint one wall lime green and another wall mint green and another . . ."

But before I have a chance to say avocado green, Dad stops me.

"Mallory, we're not going to paint your

room green, but if you'd like me to start calling you Green Bean instead of Sweet Potato, I'm happy to do that."

I frown. "I don't want to be a green bean."

Mom laughs. "How about the Queen of Green?"

I nod my head like I approve of that idea. "Maybe I can make T-shirts for Cheeseburger and me. Mine can say, *The Queen of Green,* and Cheeseburger's can say, *The Princess of Green.* I can make one for Mary Ann too. And maybe we can all wear . . . "

But before I have a chance to say matching crowns, Dad puts his fingers to my lips. "Shhh," he says as he turns out the light. "We've talked about going green enough for one day."

Mom bends down and kisses my forehead. "And we've definitely talked enough about T-shirts."

"I am kind of sleepy," I tell Dad.

I kiss my parents good night. Then I put my head on my pillow. I snuggle up with Cheeseburger. Mom is right. For today, we've talked enough about T-shirts.

But as I close my eyes, I have a vision of my cat and my best friend and me in matching T-shirts. "I vote that tomorrow is T-shirt–making day," I whisper to my cat.

She purrs like she completely agrees.

AN EMAIL FROM MALLORY

Subject: Going Green
From: malgal
To: Anyone reading this book

If you're reading this email, chances are pretty good that you just finished reading this book. And if you did, I hope you liked going green as much as I did.

If you're considering going green, I know you're wondering how to get started. Here's an idea: Grab a friend! Cleaning up the world is a lot more fun when we all do it together. Need more help? Here are some fun-and-easy tips on going green.

Good luck!

🍀 Mallory

MALLORY McDONALD'S TOP 10
FUN AND EASY WAYS TO GO GREEN

Tip #1: Follow the three Rs: REDUCE, REUSE, RECYCLE

Tip #2: Add another *R* to the list: READ about ways to save the environment.

Tip #3: TURN OFF the water when you brush your teeth. (But don't forget to brush!)

Tip #4: SWITCH to fluorescent lightbulbs.

Tip #5: UNPLUG appliances when you're not using them.

Tip #6: SHORTEN your showers. ("In and out" is my motto.)

Tip #7: PLANT a tree.

Tip #8: BAN disposable water bottles. (I bought a really cute reusable one.)

Tip #9: WALK, BIKE, or BUS it.

Tip #10: ENLIST a friend to go green with you.

And here's one last tip: Whatever you do to go green, have fun doing it!

FOR THE BIRDS

Going green is for everyone . . . even the birds! So if you want to help our feathered friends, do what my class did and make bird feeders. It's easy!

Just follow a few simple steps.

Step #1: **CUT** the front out of a milk carton. Leave 2 inches at the bottom so that you can fill it up with bird seed.

Step #2: **PAINT or PASTE** things onto the milk carton. Go crazy decorating your bird feeder. You want it to look pretty so all the birds will want to eat out of it!

Step #3: **HANG** your new bird feeder from the limbs of a nearby tree. Simply punch a hole in the top of the milk carton and use heavy string to hang it.

Step #4: **FILL** your new bird feeder with yummy (by bird standards) bird seed.

Step #5: **WAIT and WATCH** all the birds that come to eat at the beautiful, new bird feeder you made especially for them.

Darby Creek
A division of Lerner Publishing Group, Inc.
241 First Avenue North
Minneapolis, MN 55401 U.S.A.

Website address: www.lernerbooks.com

FSC
Mixed Sources
Product group from well-managed
forests, controlled sources and
recycled wood or fiber
Cert no. BV-COC-930557
www.fsc.org
© 1996 Forest Stewardship Council

Library of Congress Cataloging-in-Publication Data

Friedman, Laurie B.
        Mallory goes green! / by Laurie Friedman ; illustrations by Jennifer Kalis.
            p.   cm.
        Summary: When Mallory is appointed to the Fern Falls Elementary
School Environmental Committee, which is deciding on class projects for the
upcoming Green Fair, she rapidly succeeds in alienating her classmates,
friends, and family by her overzealous efforts to save the planet.
        ISBN: 978-0-8225-8885-6 (trade hard cover : alk. paper)
        [1. Green movement—Fiction. 2. Environmental protection—Fiction.
3. Interpersonal relations—Fiction. 4. Schools—Fiction.] I. Kalis, Jennifer, ill.
II. Title.
PZ7.F89773Mag 2010
[Fic]—dc22   2009014503

Manufactured in the United States of America
3 — BP — 12/15/10